Little Piggies

THE O'BRIEN PRESS
DUBLIN

This little piggy went to market.
This little piggy stayed home.
This little piggy had roast beef.
This little piggy had none.

But this little piggy said,
'We we we'll have a great big party
and ask our friends to come.'

So all the little piggies in the neighbourhood

came run run running as fast as they could.

Little piggies in the party mood,

so excited at the thought of food.

One little piggy couldn't stay awake.

Two little piggies baked a cake.

Three little piggies brought the cool drink crate.

Four little piggies carried all the plates.

Five little piggies came with the sweets.

Six little piggies played hide and seek.

Seven little piggies started up a band.

Eight little piggies thought the music was grand.

Nine little piggies whistled with the beat.

Ten little piggies started to eat.

J 129, 245

No little piggies went home that night,

They were all being little piggies,

and having too much fun!

Paul Morgan was born in Leonora, Western Australia, in 1951 and grew up in the Goldfields and the north of Western Australia. He completed a Teacher's Certificate in 1970 and an Associateship in Art Teaching at Curtin University in 1980. He is married with three children. This is his first book but he hopes to write many more.

Sally Morgan was born in Perth, Western Australia, in 1951. She completed a Bachelor of Arts degree at The University of Western Australia in 1974. She also has post-graduate diplomas from The Western Australian Institute of Technology in Counselling Psychology and Computing and Library Studies. She is married with three children.

As well as writing, Sally Morgan has also established a national reputation as an artist. She has published two books for adults, *My Place*, which became an instant national best-seller, and *Wanamurraganya: The Story of Jack McPhee*.

Photograph by Krystyna Petryk.

First published in Europe by The O'Brien Press Ltd.,
20 Victoria Road, Dublin 6, Ireland.
Originally published 1991 by Fremantle Arts Centre Press
193 South Terrace (PO Box 320), South Fremantle
Western Australia, 6162

British Library Cataloguing-in-publication Data
A catalogue reference for this title is available from the British Library

ISBN 0-86278-427-1

The O'Brien Press receives assistance from
The Arts Council/An Chomhairle Ealaíon.

2 4 6 8 10 9 7 5 3 1
96 98 00 02 04 03 01 99 97 95

Consultant Editor B.R. Coffey
Designed by John Douglass
Production Manager Helen Idle
Typeset in Dom Casual by Faces, West Perth
and printed on 135gsm Matt by PK Print, Western Australia